TAP! TAP! TAP!

Written by Keith Faulkner

Illustrated by Jonathan Lambert

BARRON'S

TAP! TAP! TAP!

The sound of tapping was heard all through the forest.

"What are you tapping?"
asked Squirrel.

"Is that you tapping, Baby Beaver?"
asked Beaver, down by the waterside.

TAP! TAP! TAP!

"What's that tapping?" asked Mother Wolf.

"Is it you making that noise?"

TAP! TAP! TAP!

"Fawn, is that you tapping?" called Doe, looking for her baby.

TAP! TAP! TAP!

"Who's that tapping?" asked Brown Bear. "Is it you, Cub?"

"Finished!" Woodpecker
said, flying down.
"Come and see," he added.

... and up

... and up

... and up!

"Oh! It's Woodpecker that has been tapping. He's been carving a Totem Pole!" they all cried.

All the animals
went to the other
side of the dead tree
and looked up.....